Child Listen and Look

THE SOUND WE FOUND

For our husbands and families for their support.
For the children we have worked with who have inspired us.

First published 2020 by Burton Mayers Books, www.burtonmayersbooks.com

Text copyright © Rhian Hoccom, Lisa Farquhar and Hélène Somerville

Illustration copyright © Abi de Montfort

Cover design and book design by Nought Design, www.noughtdesign.com

ISBN 9781916212640

With special thanks to:

Our speech and language therapy colleagues in the cleft palate world for seeding the idea for th[...]

Jacki Pearce for believing in us and the team at e3p for supporting the project.

For more information about the authors and organisations linked to the content of this book, please turn to the back page.

HERE ARE A FEW IDEAS TO GET THE MOST OUT OF SHARING THIS BOOK

- Keep distractions to a minimum.

- Use gentle sounds.

- Your child *does not need* to copy the sounds, though they may join in.

- Sitting face to face with your child will let them *see* the sounds as you make them.

- Remember anyone can read this book with your child.

- Why not try sharing this book in front of a mirror? Now turn the page and off you go!

Up up up for a sound play day,
hop hop hop I'm on my way.

I look at mum, she makes a sound...
p p p is the sound she found.

fff my spoon moves fast,
fff a plane zooms past.

I look at mum, she makes a sound...
fff is the sound she found.

Tiptoe tiptoe, playing hide and seek with Ted, tiptoe tiptoe, he is hiding in my bed.

I look at mum, she makes a sound...
t t t is the sound she found.

Flitter flitter flutter, a butterfly in the park,
woof woof woof, we hear the dogs bark.

I look at mum, she makes a sound...
fff is the sound she found.

Seesaw seesaw high and low,
push the swing and whoosh I go.

I look at mum she makes a sound...
sh sh sh is the sound she found.

Water from the tap says drip drip drop,
bubbles in the bath say pip pip pop.

I look at mum, she makes a sound...
p p p is the sound she found.

Turn turn turn, the pages of my book,
tweet tweet tweet, a bird mum, look!

I look at mum, she makes a sound...
t t t is the sound she found.

Lots of sounds I have heard,
by themselves and in a word.

One day soon my sounds will come,
until then, **more sound play** mum!

THE AUTHORS

Rhian Hoccom

Lisa Farquhar

Hélène Somerville

For more information about the authors and books in the series, please visit

www.burtonmayersbooks.com/the-sound-we-found

WE HOPE YOU ENJOYED THIS BOOK.
LOOK OUT FOR MORE BOOKS IN THE SERIES!